# LITTLE DOG MOON

Story by Maxine Trottier
Paintings by Laura Fernandez & Rick Jacobson

Stoddart
Kids
TORONTO • NEW YORK

Published in Canada in 2000 by
Stoddart Kids,
a division of Stoddart Publishing Co. Limited
34 Lesmill Road
Toronto, ON M3B 2T6
Tel (416) 445-3333 FAX (416) 445-5967
E-mail Customer.Service@ccmailgw.genpub.com

Published in the United States in 2000 by
Stoddart Kids,
a division of Stoddart Publishing Co. Limited
180 Varick Street, 9th Floor
New York, New York 10014
Toll free 1-800-805-1083
E-mail gdsinc@genpub.com

Distributed in Canada by
General Distribution Services
325 Humber College Blvd.,
Toronto, ON M9W 7C3
Tel (416) 213-1919 FAX (416) 213-1917
E-mail Customer.Service@ccmailgw.genpub.com

Distributed in the United States by
General Distribution Services
85 River Rock Drive, Suite 202
Buffalo, New York 14207
Toll free 1-800-805-1083
E-mail gdsinc@genpub.com

**Canadian Cataloguing in Publication Data**

Trottier, Maxine
Little dog Moon

ISBN 0-7737-3220-9

I. Fernandez, Laura.  II. Jacobson, Rick.
III. Title.

PS8589.R685L57 2000   jC813'.54   C99-932575-2
PZ7.T76Li 2000

*Two Tibetan children trying to reach Nepal, are assisted
by a small dog who leads them through the mountains to safety.*

THE CANADA COUNCIL | LE CONSEIL DES ARTS
FOR THE ARTS | DU CANADA
SINCE 1957 | DEPUIS 1957

*We acknowledge for their financial support of our
publishing program the Canada Council, the Ontario Arts
Council, and the Government of Canada through the
Book Publishing Industry Development Program (BPIDP).*

Printed in Hong Kong

*To Kathryn,*
*for the books and the laughter*
*and the love of dogs we share.*
— MAXINE

*For our children.*
— LAURA AND RICK

Early one morning, the sun rose over the tops of the mountains in Tibet. Pale light spilled across the valley and tinted the walls of an ancient monastery with soft rose. The monks who lived there had been up for many hours, chanting and praying. Now they went about their tasks and the sounds that fill busy mornings everywhere drifted into the thin, mountain air.

Tenzin stepped outside to sweep the stairs. A little dog followed him. There were other dogs in the monastery, but this one, Moon, had claimed the young monk as her own. She followed him down shadowy halls or lay close, as still as a small, stone lion, when he shut his eyes in prayer. At night, when Tenzin settled in his narrow bed, Moon curled around his feet. There in the monastery, life was filled with peace.

Like all the monastery dogs, Moon wandered the hillsides. With her heavy coat she did not mind the wind or cold. Her wide, flat feet carried her over the ground in winter. Tenzin would watch her climb higher and higher until finally she disappeared beyond the rise. He did not worry. She knew the mountain paths better than any other dog.

Each day passed, quiet and calm. Then one evening, as Tenzin sat thinking near the monastery door, he heard a sound. Moon heard it as well. She lifted her head and stared into the darkness. Slowly, two children walked out of the mist.

Tenzin had seen such children before, though few were this young. They tried to cross to the freedom that waited in Nepal. Hurrying through the night, they hoped to slip past soldiers who guarded the border.

"Are we there?" asked the girl who held tightly to a little boy's hand. "Are we in Nepal?"

"No. Not yet," answered Tenzin, unable to tell them the journey was still long and dangerous. As Moon sniffed their legs, he led them inside.

The monks brought the children to the fire. Hot soup was served and the girl talked quietly as she ate.

Their mother had sent them away many days before. "You must cross the mountains and leave Tibet," she had said. "There you will be free."

She dressed them in layers of heavy sweaters and put thick socks on their feet. She knew her children should leave in winter when the passes were not so carefully watched, but she feared they would be lost forever in the cruel storms and deep snow.

"Will you come, too, Mother?" her son asked.

"Of course I will come," she answered quietly. The mother could not meet her daughter's sad eyes. "Until then, you must do this for me." She pulled out a roll of cloth and shook it loose.

"A prayer flag," said the boy. He loved to hear the snap of flags in the wind.

"You must keep this close to your heart," said his mother. She folded the flag and tucked it deep within his sweaters, next to his skin. "When you reach Nepal, tie it to a temple and let it fly in the wind. The prayers I send with you will lift to the sky and come back to me. Then I will know you are safe."

The children had walked forever it seemed, following the stony roads that wound through the mountains. At last they had come to the monastery. Tenzin shook his head as he watched them nodding sleepily over their soup bowls. They had journeyed so far and would probably go no further. "They will be turned back," he whispered to himself.

All that night Tenzin lay awake, thinking of what he must do. Before dawn he rose and prayed with the other monks. Then, with Moon and the children at his heels, he went to the monastery doors.

"The guards will not let you through," he said. "You must not use the mountain road."

"We know no other way," the girl told him.

"Perhaps not, but Moon does," answered Tenzin. He knelt down to stroke the long hair away from the little dog's eyes. "Take them. Show them the path."

Moon looked up into Tenzin's face for a moment, then she started off toward the mountains. The girl held onto her brother's hand and the boy held onto the dog. Tenzin watched them for a long while. Just before the three figures disappeared over the rise, he was certain that he saw Moon's small head turn to look back at him. Then they were gone.

Each day Tenzin scanned the hillsides, but he did not see Moon. He prayed and went to his studies. At night he slept alone with an ache in his heart where once peace had been. Days became weeks. Summer turned into fall, and when winter came, the monastery was locked in its icy hold.

One chilly, spring morning, Tenzin walked into the sunshine. Icicles dripped from the monastery eaves and patches of wet earth glittered on the mountainside. Then, one of the patches moved and a bark rang out! A small shape walked slowly down the slope. Tenzin raced forward to meet Moon. He gathered her up and carried her home to the monastery.

The monks rejoiced as they stroked and petted Moon. Her coat was dirty and matted and the pads of her feet were sore. As Tenzin scratched her ears and neck, he felt something. Beneath the dog's long hair was a roll of cloth. Tenzin untied it and shook it loose.

"The prayer flag," he whispered in surprise.

With Moon and the monks following, he went outside. He carefully fastened the flag to a line so that it would catch the wind.

Late that night Tenzin lay in his bed. Moon was curled around his feet, quiet but watchful. Suddenly, she lifted her head, listening to something that only a dog might hear. It was a sound as sweet as the distant laughter of happy children, a sound as soft as a mother's smile. The sound drifted away like smoke into the darkness. Little dog Moon lowered her head and closed her eyes. And wrapped in peace once more, she and Tenzin slept.

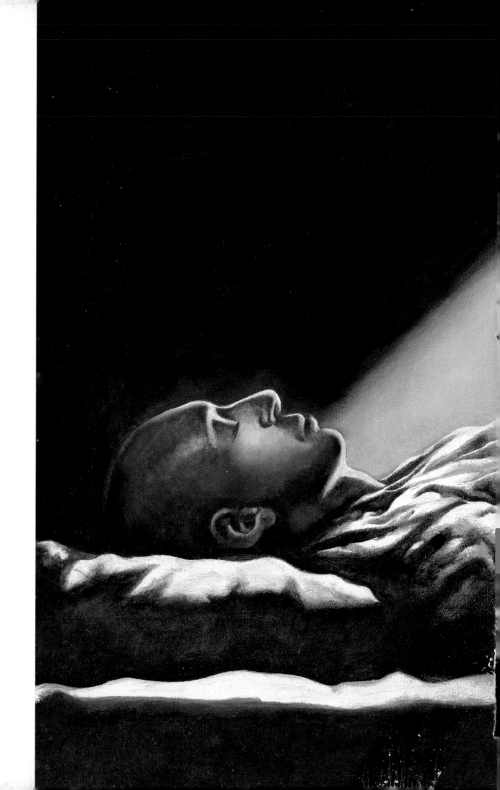

# Author's Notes

Little Moon, the dog in this story, is a Tibetan terrier. The breed is a very old one and has an interesting past. It is said that the dogs were originally kept as companions in the isolated monasteries in what would one day be called the Lost Valley of Tibet. Set deep in the Himalayan Mountains, the trek to and from such places was perilous. The dogs were intelligent, sure-footed, had an unfailing sense of direction, and were said to bring good luck. Like Moon, they learned the secret ways in and out of the mountains. They were never sold because doing so would "sell one's good luck." The dogs were, however, given as gifts to people held in high esteem. One of these gifts was eventually brought to England and became the foundation of Tibetan terriers as we know them.

With their double coats of wool and hair, and wide "snowshoe" feet, the dogs were perfectly suited to their rugged life. They were called "little people" by the Tibetans and, as members of the family, were expected to do their share of work. As a result, they became herd dogs and watch dogs. They have no terrier traits other than their size. Today, with their calm, steady natures and high intelligence, they are well-loved pets in the families whose lives they share.

*Little Dog Moon* is about bravery and strength of spirit. It is also about family, sacrifice, and the wonderful things that love can bring about. Great courage is often necessary to seek out things that are important to you, even if you are lucky enough to live with the priceless gift of freedom. But there are many people in the world who will never know this gift. We all deserve the right to speak our mind, to read the books we wish to read, to practice our religion, and to live without fear. These are the things that parents wish for their children. As a writer and an educator, my hopes for you — for all children — are the same.